PIG DETECTIVES
CERDOS DETECTIVES

Rosie Albright

Traducción al español: Eduardo Alamán

PowerKiDS press

New York

Published in 2012 by The Rosen Publishing Group, Inc.
29 East 21st Street, New York, NY 10010

First Edition

Editor: Joanne Randolph   Traducción al español: Eduardo Alamán
Book Design: Kate Laczynski

Photo Credits: Cover, pp. 16, 19, 20, 24 (hooves) David Silverman/Getty Images; pp. 5, 6, 9, 10, 14–15, 24 (bomb, snout, truffles) Shutterstock.com; pp. 12–13 Olivier Laban-Mattei/AFP/ Getty Images; p. 23 iStockphoto/Thinkstock.

Library of Congress Cataloging-in-Publication Data

Albright, Rosie.
  [Pig detectives. Spanish & English]
Pig detectives = Cerdos detectives / Rosie Albright. — 1st ed.
    p. cm. — (Animal detectives = Detectives del reino animal)
Includes index.
ISBN 978-1-4488-6718-9 (library binding)
I. Title. II. Title: Cerdos detectives.
SF395.5.A5318 2012
636.4′0886—dc23
                                        2011027096

Web Sites: Due to the changing nature of Internet links, PowerKids Press has developed an online list of Web sites related to the subject of this book. This site is updated regularly. Please use this link to access the list: www.powerkidslinks.com/andt/pig/

Manufactured in the United States of America

CPSIA Compliance Information: Batch #WW12PK: For Further Information contact Rosen Publishing, New York, New York at 1-800-237-9932

CONTENTS

Meet the Pig   4

Pigs at Work   12

On the Case!   22

Words to Know   24

Index   24

CONTENIDO

Conoce a los cerdos   4

En el trabajo   12

¡Un caso resuelto!   22

Palabras que debes saber   24

Índice   24

Pigs are smart animals. Pigs can live on farms or be kept as pets.

Los cerdos son muy inteligentes. Los cerdos pueden vivir en granjas o como mascotas.

5

Pigs have a great sense of smell. They do not see very well, though.

Los cerdos tienen un buen sentido del olfato. Pero su sentido de la vista no es muy bueno.

Pigs use their noses to hunt for food. Then they dig up the food.

Los cerdos usan su **hocico**, o nariz, para buscar comida. Luego, desentierran la comida.

Pigs dig mostly with their **hooves**. They also use their strong **snouts** for digging.

Los cerdos excavan con sus **pezuñas**. Además usan sus fuertes hocicos para excavar.

People have been training pigs for hundreds of years. People use trained pigs to find **truffles**.

Los cerdos han sido entrenados desde hace cientos de años. Los cerdos se usan para encontrar **trufas**.

Truffles are mushrooms. They grow under the ground.

Las trufas son hongos. Las trufas crecen bajo tierra.

People also train pigs to sniff out **bombs**. They are used for this job in airports.

Los cerdos también aprenden a olfatear **bombas**. Estos cerdos trabajan en aeropuertos.

Pigs sniff out land mines in Israel. They have been used in Africa, too.

En Israel, los cerdos olfatean minas terrestres. También hacen ese trabajo en África.

Land mines kill hundreds of people every year. Land mines are used during wars.

Las minas terrestres matan a cientos de personas cada año. Las minas terrestres se usan en las guerras.

Pigs and their noses are on the case!

¡Los cerdos y sus hocicos resuelven el caso!

Words to Know / Palabras que debes saber

bomb / (la) bomba

hooves / (las) pezuñas

snout / (el) hocico

truffles / (las) trufas

Index

A
airports, 17

B
bombs, 17

F
food, 8

H
hooves, 11

Índice

A
aeropuertos, 17

B
bombas, 17

C
comida, 8

P
pezuñas, 11